Music in My Soul

Written by
Marian Schmitt

Illustrated by
Louis J. Schmitt

AMP&RSAND, INC.

Chicago • New Orleans

ISBN 9781-4507-0622-390000

PUBLISHED BY

AMP&RSAND, INC.

Chicago · New Orleans

1050 North State Street
Chicago, IL 60610

203 Finland Place
New Orleans, LA 70131

www.ampersandworks.com

Printed in U.S.A.

This book is dedicated to
our friends and family who
put music in our souls and
love in our hearts

"How'd I get my name?" I asked my mama.
"You're named after a very famous jazz musician,
Louis Armstrong," she said smiling.
"Why did you name me after him?"
"When you were born and the first time
I heard you wail, I knew that you had

music in your soul."

My sister, the pest, said that I was named after LouisiAna.
I just ignored her.

"How did I get music in my soul?"
"It's all around you," Mama said. "Think about it."

I thought about it.

I thought about
the clapping games on playgrounds ...
Miss Mary Mack, Mack, Mack
All dressed in black, black, black ...

I thought about
the tunes of Double Dutch
as ropes click-clacked on the ground.

I thought about
Mardi Gras parades and the excitement, and
the sounds of bands growing louder and louder
as they came closer to us.

I thought about
church and the songs of praise
sung by gospel singers
in colorful robes.

I thought about the joyous sounds, waving handkerchiefs, and twirling umbrellas of a second-line.

I thought about

the whirring sounds of the street car
and the clanging of the bell as it rolled
down the tracks on St. Charles Avenue.

I thought about the festive sounds of the carousel at City Park as I ran to get on one of the flying horses that went up and down.

I thought about

those days of summer when we'd sit on the levee
listening to the paddle wheeler's calliope as it
cruised down the muddy Mississippi.

I thought about the chiming bells of St. Louis Cathedral and the people stopping and listening to their beautiful sounds.

I thought about
the times we peaked through the open doors of Preservation Hall and saw gray-haired musicians playing their worn out instruments.

I ran to my mama.
"Oh, Mama you're right!
**I do have music
in my soul!**
And when I grow up, I want
to share my music so other
people can have music in
their souls, too."

New Orleans is a city rich in wonderful sounds that have inspired people for generations. The city's history is full of musicians who have reached world-wide fame, including Louis Armstrong, after whom our airport is named. Some historians believe that New Orleans is the birthplace of Jazz even though other cities also make that claim.

From the call of seagulls at the Lakefront, to the busy tourists conversing about our unique cuisine, to the joyful laughter of happy children, to the musicians performing in Jackson Square, to the music being played on almost every downtown corner, there are sounds to be heard. We urge you to listen and hope that what you hear will bring music to your soul.

Marian Schmitt was born in New Orleans and lived on the Westbank in Algiers. There she taught in the public elementary schools for 40 years. Her love of New Orleans, its customs, culture and its joyful, vibrant children led her to write this book. In it she portrays the musical charm of the city she loved so much.

Marian's nephew, Louis Schmitt, is an artist.
His love of New Orleans is reflected in his art.

AMAZING PARTNERSHIPS

BY VIRGINIA LOH-HAGAN

45TH PARALLEL PRESS

Published in the United States of America by Cherry Lake Publishing Group
Ann Arbor, Michigan
www.cherrylakepublishing.com

Reading Adviser: Beth Walker Gambro, MS Ed., Reading Consultant, Yorkville, IL
Book Designer: Melinda Millward

Photo Credits: Cover: © Jezbennett/Dreamstime; Page 1: © Jezbennett/Dreamstime; Page 5: © Wirestock/Dreamstime; Page 6: © Suateracar/Dreamstime, © Artush/Shutterstock; Page 7: © Michele Burgess/Adobe Stock; Page 8: © Stu Porter/Shutterstock, © Gillian Holliday/Shutterstock; Page 9: © Jezbennett/Dreamstime; Page 10: © pjmalsbury/iStockphoto; Page 12: © Mike Bauer/Shutterstock, © willtu/Adobe Stock; Page 13: © Marty Wakat/Shutterstock; Page 14: © willtu/Adobe Stock; Page 16: © diveivanov/Adobe Stock, © Song Heming/Dreamstime; Page 17: © Orlandin/Dreamstime; Page 18: © blue-sea.cz/Shutterstock, © cbpix/Shutterstock; Page 19: © Daniel Lamborn/Shutterstock; Page 20: © Kurit afshen/Shutterstock; Page 22: © Steven Ellingson/Shutterstock, © inkwelldodo/Shutterstock; Page 23: © Frantisek Dulik/Shutterstock

Graphic Element Credits: Cover, multiple interior pages: © paprika/Shutterstock, © Silhouette Lover/Shutterstock, © Daria Rosen/Shutterstock, © Wi_Stock/Shutterstock

Library of Congress Cataloging-in-Publication Data

Names: Loh-Hagan, Virginia, author.
Title: Amazing partnershiA / written by Virginia Loh-Hagan.
Description: Ann Arbor, Michigan : Cherry Lake Publishing, [2023] | Series: Wild Wicked Wonderful Express. | Audience: Grades 2-3 | Summary: "Which animals have a bond that can't be broken? This book explores the wild, wicked, and wonderful world of animal partnershiA. Series is developed to aid struggling and reluctant young readers with engaging high-interest content, considerate text, and clear visuals. Includes table of contents, glossary with simplified pronunciations, index, sidebars, and author biographies"—Provided by publisher.
Identifiers: LCCN 2022042701 | ISBN 9781668920749 (paperback) | ISBN 9781668919729 (hardcover) | ISBN 9781668922071 (ebook) | ISBN 9781668923405 (pdf)
Subjects: LCSH: Symbiosis—Juvenile literature. | Mutualism (Biology)—Juvenile literature.
Classification: LCC QL756.8 .L64 2023 | DDC 591.7/85—dc23/eng/20220916
LC record available at httA://lccn.loc.gov/2022042701

Cherry Lake Publishing Group would like to acknowledge the work of the Partnership for 21st Century Learning. a Network of Battelle for Kids. Please visit http://www.battelleforkids.org/networks/p21 for more information.

Printed in the United States of America

About the Author

Dr. Virginia Loh-Hagan is an author, university professor, former classroom teacher, and curriculum designer. She lives in San Diego and has an extreme partnership with her very tall husband and very naughty dogs.

Table of Contents

Introduction 4

Zebras and Ostriches 6

Cattle Egrets and Hippos 8

Green Sea Turtles and Yellow Tang Fish 12

Goby Fish and Pistol Shrimp 16

Clownfish and Sea Anemones 18

Ants and Aphids 22

Consider This! 24
Glossary 24
Index 24

Introduction

Animals team up. They work together. Animal partners need each other to **survive**. Survive means to stay alive. They **benefit** from their partnership. Benefit means to get something good.

Some animals have extreme partnerships. Some animal partnerships are odder than others. These are the most exciting partnerships in the animal world!

Zebras and ostriches work together to stay safe!

Zebras and Ostriches

Zebras and ostriches roam together. Ostriches are the tallest and largest birds. They have the biggest eyes. They see far. They see from a high point. They see details very clearly. They're fast. But they also depend on zebras. Zebras have a great sense of smell. Together, ostriches and zebras see and smell **predators**. Predators are animals that hunt other animals for food.

Zebras call to each other when they sense predators. They warn others to run away. Ostriches know zebras' alarm call. They run away too.

Zebras and ostriches live on savannas.
Savannas are warm grasslands.

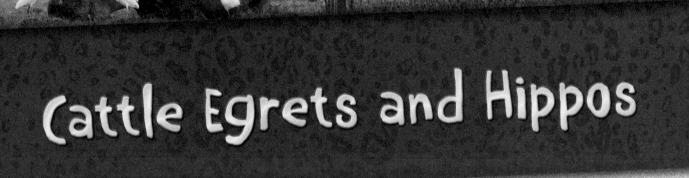

Cattle Egrets and Hippos

Adult hippos are dangerous. They charge and attack. But baby hippos are **vulnerable** to predators. Vulnerable means open to danger.

Birds called cattle egrets help baby hippos. They serve as a lookout. They ride on hippos' backs. They can see a long way. They spot predators.

Cattle egrets also help hippos by eating harmful bugs off them.

Cattle egrets and hippos are both native to Africa.

Cattle egrets benefit when hippos travel together. The hippos stir up bugs. Cattle egrets eat the bugs. They also get a free ride. This saves their energy.

When Animals Attack!

Coyotes and badgers don't get along. But they both eat squirrels and prairie dogs. They work together to hunt.

Coyotes are great runners. Badgers are great diggers. They combine their skills. Coyotes chase the **prey**. Prey are animals hunted for food. They tire out the prey. The prey then hide underground. Then badgers come to help. They dig the prey out of their underground homes.

Green Sea Turtles and Yellow Tang Fish

Green sea turtles can live 80 years. They need to stay healthy to live that long. Yellow tang fish help.

Algae grow on sea turtles' shells. Algae are plants that grow on or in water. The algae can be dangerous for sea turtles.

Yellow tang fish live in tropical coral reefs.
Sea turtles can live all over the world!

13

The coral reef can be like a cleaning station.

They can't swim as fast with algae on their shells. Predators can catch slow sea turtles.

Yellow tang fish eat algae. They eat the algae right off the sea turtles!

Humans
Do What?!?

Humans and **bacteria** need each other. Bacteria are tiny living things that live inside and outside people and animals. Bacteria need humans to live. Humans need bacteria to stay healthy. Dave Whitlock is a chemical engineer. He hasn't showered in more than 12 years! He wants to keep helpful bacteria on his skin. He was inspired by a horse. He saw a horse roll around in the dirt. It gave itself a dirt bath. Horses do this to keep their coats healthy. They also do this to protect their skin.

Goby Fish and Pistol Shrimp

Goby fish and pistol shrimp share a home. Pistol shrimp live in burrows. They live under the ocean floor.

Their homes can cave in. That might bury goby fish. But pistol shrimp will dig them out.

Goby fish protect pistol shrimp. Pistol shrimp can't see. Goby fish see very well. They signal pistol shrimp to hide.

Pistol shrimp build burrows
big enough for goby fish.

Clownfish and Sea Anemones

Sea anemones have **tentacles**. Tentacles are long, flexible arms. Sea anemones don't move as they hunt. Instead, they use their tentacles. One tentacle sticks to a rock. They use the others to sting and stun prey. The sea anemones then move the prey into their mouths.

Clownfish need protection. They can't swim fast. They partner with sea anemones.

Clownfish can't get hurt by sea anemones.
Mucus on their skin protects them.

Clownfish clean sea anemones.

They hide in their tentacles. Clownfish are protected from the stings of sea anemones.

Clownfish also protect sea anemones. Butterfly fish eat sea anemones. But clownfish chase butterfly fish away.

Did You Know...?

- Egrets don't just ride on hippos. They ride on the backs of other large animals. Partners include rhinos, elephants, and horses.

- Zebras also partner with birds called oxpeckers. These birds eat **parasites** off zebras. Parasites are animals that survive by living on another animal. But sometimes oxpeckers create more trouble. They can pick at cuts on the zebra's skin. This invites more parasites.

Ants and Aphids

Aphids are pests. They eat the sugary fluid inside plants. They poop a lot. Their poop is sweet. It's called **honeydew**.

Ants love honeydew. So, they capture aphids. Ants take good care of aphids. They protect them.

Both animals benefit. Ants feed on honeydew. Aphids trade their freedom for protection.

Ants stop disease from spreading to aphid herds. They get rid of the sick aphids.

Consider This!

Take a Position! Some scientists like to study animal relationships. What if scientists put different animals together to study them? Think about the advantages and disadvantages. Do you think this is the right thing to do? Why or why not?

Think About It! Animals and humans collaborate and compete. Collaborate means to work with others. Compete means to go against someone in order to win. When is it important to collaborate? When is it important to compete? This book focused on animal collaborations. Think of ways in which animals compete instead of collaborate.

Learn More
- **Book:** Cohn, Scotti, and Shennen Bersani (illustrator). Animal Partners. Mt. Pleasant, SC: Arbordale Publishing, 2015.
- **Show:** Unlikely Animal Friends from National Geographic (2012-2019)

Glossary

algae (AL-jee) small rootless, stemless plants that grow on or in water

bacteria (bak-TIHR-ee-uh) tiny living things that live inside and outside people and animals

benefit (BEH-nuh-fit) to gain something positive or good

honeydew (HUHN-ee-doo) aphid poop that is really sweet

parasites (PAR-uh-sytz) animals that live on or in other animals

predators (PREH-duh-turz) animals that hunt other animals for food

prey (PRAY) animals hunted for food

survive (sur-VYV) stay alive

tentacles (TEN-tih-kuhlz) long, flexible arms found on some animals

vulnerable (VUHL-nuh-ruh-buhl) unsafe; open to danger

Index

algae, 12, 13, 14
ants, 22–23
aphids, 22–23

baby animals, 8
bacteria, 15
badgers, 11
birds, 5, 6–7, 8–10, 21
butterfly fish, 20

cattle egrets, 8–10, 21
cleaning and grooming, 9, 10, 12–14, 15, 20, 21
clownfish, 18–20
coyotes, 11

defenses, 6, 8, 16, 18–20, 22

egrets, 8–10, 21

fish, 12–14, 16–17, 18–20

goby fish, 16–17
grasslands, 7
green sea turtles, 12–14
grooming and cleaning, 9, 10, 12–14, 15, 20, 21

habitats, 7, 10, 11, 13, 16–17, 18–20
hippos, 8–10, 21
horses, 15

humans, 15

insects, 22–23

life spans, 5, 12

ostriches, 5, 6–7
oxpeckers, 21

parasites, 21
pistol shrimp, 16–17
prairie dogs, 11
predators and prey, 6, 8, 11, 14, 18
protection, 6, 8, 16, 18–20, 22

savannas, 7
sea anemones, 18–20
sea turtles, 12–14
senses, 6, 16
shrimp, 16–17
squirrels, 11

tentacles, 18–20
turtles, 12–14

yellow tang fish, 12–14

zebras, 5, 6–7, 21

24